# MERLIN & THE SNAKE'S EGG

Poems by Leslie Norris

Illustrated by Ted Lewin

THE VIKING PRESS
NEW YORK

First Edition
Copyright © Leslie Norris, 1978
Illustrations copyright © Ted Lewin, 1978
All rights reserved
First published in 1978 by The Viking Press
625 Madison Avenue, New York, N.Y. 10022
Published simultaneously in Canada by
Penguin Books Canada Limited
Printed in U.S.A.
1   2   3   4   5   82   81   80   79   78

Library of Congress Cataloging in Publication Data
Norris, Leslie,   Merlin & the snake's egg.
    Summary: A collection of poems about such everyday
events as buying a puppy, playing football, and
collecting frogs.
    [1.   English poetry]   I.   Lewin, Ted.   II.   Title.
PR6027.O44M4      821'.9'14      77-15558
ISBN 0-670-47191-7

# Contents

# WALKING

*SMALL FROGS*

We climbed to the pond,
I and my cousin,
And frogs by the swarm
And bundle and dozen

Came bustling down
The coal-dark hill.
So many frogs
We both stood still.

Each black frog
Was spider-small,
Small as clover,
As a fingernail.

Small as raindrops
They hurried through the grass
As we stood watching
The baby frogs pass.

And two little frogs
From the pilgrimage
I put in prison
In my fingers' cage.

They were so light,
Their skin so cool,
I could not feel them
There at all

4

But watched them sitting
On my hand,
Two alive creatures
Of water and land,

Their legs no longer
Than a drawing-pin,
Their wide mouths drinking
The warm air in,

Their skin like paper,
Their tiny paws,
The brilliant particles
Of their eyes,

And put them down
And watched them go,
All knowing something
We can't know.

They'd lived in water!
They'd grown four legs!
What a world we live in
For boys and frogs.

## THE PARK AT EVENING

I like the park best at evening, on a cool day,
When the children's voices sound thin and sweet,
Hanging in the air like shreds of clouds.
And birches at the edge of the park grow frail,
Grow misty like a line of smoke, low and small
At the very edge of our eyesight,
At the edge of the park.

I like it when hiding children
Come running from behind trees and bushes.
"All in, all in," they call.
Just as the parkkeeper rings his bell,
Sending them home, where their mothers
In lit kitchens are cooking sausages,
Growing the smallest bit anxious,
As the park turns gently into evening.

## KEVIN SCORES!

Kevin flicks the ball sideways, leaning
From it, letting it roll
Away, smoothly. He knows Tom is sprinting
Up from defence for it, down
The touchline, so he moves seriously beyond
The centre-back, hoping the ball will come
Over, perfectly, within the reach
Of his timed leap, so he can dive upward,
Feet pointed, arms balancing, soaring,
Arched like a hawk for the stab of his head at the goal.

He has seen it often, Law
And Osgood on the telly,
How they wait hungrily
Under the ball floating over,
Then the great poise of the leap,
Almost too late you'd think,
Like great cats hunting,
Or sleek, muscular sharks,
Leaping beyond gravity, up, up!
Then the sharp snap of the head
And the white ball coldly in the net.

Kevin waits by the far post, willing
Tom to get the ball over.
He feels slack and alone, he can see
David in goal, elbows tensely bent, fingers
Stretched for catching in his old woollen gloves.
Tom sways inside the back, he takes two
Short steps, he swings
His left foot, and the ball lifts
Perfectly, perfectly,
Within the bound of Kevin's timed leap.
He is drawn to it, he straightens
In a slow, upward dive, and he bends back,
Eyes rapt on the crossed ball he rises
To meet, and *now*
The sharp snap of his head
And the white ball coldly past the plunging David.

As he runs downfield he knows his face is laughing.

## SWAN

Swan, unbelievable bird, a cloud floating,
Arrangement of enormous white chrysanthemums
In a shop kept by angels, feathery statue
Carved from the fall of snow,

You are not too proud to take the crusts we offer.
You are so white that clear water stains you
And I am ashamed that you have to swim
Here, where cigarette cartons hang in the lake,

And the plastic containers that held our ice cream.
Now you bend your neck strong as a hawser
And I see your paddles like black rubber
Open and close as you move the webs of your swimming.

About you the small ducks, the coots, and the timid
Water-rails keep their admiring distances. Do not hurry.
Take what you need of our thrown bread, white swan,
Before you drift away, a cloud floating.

# WOODSPELLS

## SPELL OF THE RAINGODS

We are the Raingods, we are the clouds,
Gathering and muttering and rumbling together,
Listening to little things praying for wet weather—
        I'm OOM
        I'm BOOM
        and I'm TARAH!

We are howling through the mountains
We are shrieking through the plain,
Billowing and bellowing and ripe with rain—
        I'm OOM
        I'm BOOM
        and I'm TARAH!

We rule the running rivers
And we plump the growing grain
And all the trees are ours, for we bring them rain—
I'm OOM
I'm BOOM
and I'm TARAH!

*SPELL OF THE RAIN*

Falling
    the small drops,
The meek rain
    stopping at nothing,
The empty rain
    filling all stomachs,
The tiny rain
    making rivers,
    torrents,
    ferocious oceans,
The weak rain
    nourishing tall forests,
The clear rain
    greening the leaves,
The small drops
    are falling . . .

## SPELL OF THE SEEDS

A great oak
In an acorn,
Groves of pine trees
In one cone;
Come Spring, wave your green wand.

In a bright berry
The hawthorn,
So too
Is holly born;
Come Spring, wave your green wand.

Dry seeds, light,
Lighter than hair,
But great forests
Are waiting there;
Soon  Spring, wave your green wand.

## SPELL OF THE GODDESS

I am the four-in-one,
  the single Goddess
Whose separate changes bring
  poverty or riches,
Whose voices sing the truth
  of cold or kindness.

See me at first as Spring,
  the always welcome,
With arms full of primroses
  and voice of larksong.
I dress the trees in green,
  I make the woods young.

Now I am glowing Summer:
  all through my days
Shadows rich as velvet
  sit under trees,
Gnats dance in the sunlight,
  in the warm haze.

But when I am Autumn
  I change my dress.
I walk in gold and red
  as plenty's Goddess.
Berries are ripe and plump, windfalls
  lie in the grass.

Lastly, I'm Winter's Witch,
  hard as a bone.
The touch of my cold hand
  turns water to stone.
I fill the dying year
  with the forest's moan.

I can split a great oak
  with the ice of my breath,
Quietly slaughter the leaves
  with my frost's stealth.
I bring to the shuddering wood
  its annual death.

I am the four-in-one,
    The single Goddess
Who comes to the turning year
    in four disguises,
Whose voices sing the truth
    of cold or kindness.

## SPELL OF THE MOON

Owl floats through the midnight wood
His terrible voice.
Small creatures alive on the ground
Keep still as ice,
Afraid their bones will be snapped
In his talon's vice.

But the moon hangs in the air,
In the tree's arms,
And she throws on trees and ground
Her silver charms,
Healing the fear of the dark
And night's alarms.

The fox to his lair in the dark
Through shadows will slip,
The shrew and the mole and the vole
To safety creep,
And the moon ride silent and high.
And the wood's asleep.

*SPELL OF THE WOODS*

Listen, the trees are singing
And the wood is full of voices.
From the lake's edge
Trembles the willow's song
And poplars
Fly high, silver whispers
On the carrying air.
All the trees are singing.

Sing then, alder and ash!
Sing, mellow-sounding beech!
And you small animals,
Keep still among the roots;
Birds, do not shout your notes
From any thicket!
Keep silent now while the wood
Makes its ancient music
And the trees sing, all the trees sing.

Oh, the wood is a great choir.
From a green dark
The deep oaks chant
In their mossy voices
And the wind
Sounds its sobbing cellos
In the elm trees.
The trees toss aloft their branches
As they sing, as loudly the trees sing.

# SOME DOGS

BUYING A PUPPY

"Bring an old towel," said Pa,
"And a scrap of meat from the pantry.
We're going out in the car, you and I,
Into the country."

I did as he said, although
I couldn't see why he wanted
A scrap of meat and an old towel.
Into the sun we pointed

Our Ford, over the green hills.
Pa sang. Larks bubbled in the sky.
I took with me all my cards—
It was my seventh birthday.

We turned down a happy lane,
Half sunlight, half shadow,
And saw at the end a white house
In a yellow meadow.

Mrs. Garner lived there. She was tall.
She gave me a glass of milk
And showed me her black spaniel.
"Her name is Silk,"

Mrs. Garner said. "She's got
Three puppies, two black, one golden.
Come and see them." Oh,
To have one, one of my own!

"You can choose one," said Pa.
I looked at him. He wasn't joking.
I could scarcely say thank you,
I was almost choking.

It was the golden one. He slept
On my knee in the old towel
All the way home. He was tiny,
But he didn't whimper or howl,

Not once. That was a year ago,
And now I'm eight.
When I get home from school
He'll be waiting behind the gate,

Listening, listening hard,
Head raised, eyes warm and kind;
He came to me as a gift
And grew into a friend.

## THE OLD DOG'S SONG

What does the old dog say?
Well, here's another day
To sit in the sun.
And when my master's up
I'll skip around like a pup
And we'll go for a run.
But now I'll lift my head
Out of my warm bed
To greet the dawn,
Sigh gently, and slowly turn,
Slowly lie down again,
And gently yawn.

All night I've kept an eye
Open protectingly
In case of danger.
If anything had gone wrong,
I would have raised my strong
Voice in anger.
But all was safe and still.
The sun's come over the hill,
No need for warning.
When he comes down the stair
I shall be waiting there
To say Good Morning.

## A MAN IN OUR VILLAGE

A man in our village,
a village high in the hills,
often among clouds,
a poor village with little money,
this man had a dog.

She was not a pretty dog.
Her coat was unkempt black and tan
and she was small and thin.
You wouldn't have looked twice at her—
unless you had noticed how closely
she stayed beside the man,
watching his every step, staying
close to his heels, watching him.
It was clear she loved the man.

The dog's eyes were brown
and very, very bright. Her name
was Betsy. Someone told me that.
I never heard anyone call her by name,
nobody patted her or fondled her ears.
Once a child bent down to speak to her
where she sat near the man
as he spoke to a friend in the street.
But she growled quietly, not in anger,
just to say she didn't want to be spoken to.
The man was just a man.

There was a high path over the hills,
a short cut to the next valley.
One day people saw the man and his dog
walk out along the path. It was winter,
the hill pools had been solid ice for a month,
the ground was as hard as a bone.
The man vanished around a bend
and his dog was as frail behind him
as his winter shadow. And soon it grew dark.

Not only evening dark, not only the natural dusk.
Clouds heavy with snow grew bleakly under the moon
and in an hour the hills, the village,
the white countryside, all lay under the muffling
snow. All night it fell. Everything
was altered. All paths were hidden under
that fallen sky. We began to worry
about the man and his little dog.

In the morning we set out over the changed hills,
in a long line, calling one to the other,
to keep in touch. Blue shadows filled
the hollows, and we swung our arms in the cold
and we shouted. All morning we searched
but we did not find them, nor any sign of them.

A bitter wind filled our eyes with tears
and we moved slowly, with great weariness,
through the deep snow. We gave up hope.
We stumbled back along the tracks we had made.

But a great shout stopped us. They were found!
We knew they were found by the joy
of the loud call, by the waving of arms
near a crop of rocks. They lay under
what shelter the rocks could have given them
and they were alive. The man could not hear us,
he was insensible with cold. But his little dog
had crept and curled herself over his heart
and kept him warm. She had saved his life.
We brought them down, step by step, through snow,
and into a house blazing with comfort.
We praised the little dog, made much of her,
gave her warm milk to drink, for the first time
spoke her name.

When summer came again and the hills
turned kind and pink with heather,
the man sold his dog to a passing visitor.
He sold her, although she had saved his life.
Would you have done that, would you?
I didn't think anyone could have done that.

# FROM DARKNESS UNDERGROUND

## THE COLLIER LADDIE

When my grandpa was a little boy
Many and many a year ago
He hadn't much time to laugh and play
For he was a collier laddie.

When my grandpa was but eight years old
Many and many a year ago
He went down the mine to cut the coal
For he was a collier laddie.

He'd rise in the morning before the sun
Many and many a year ago
And he wouldn't get home until day was done
Like many a collier laddie.

He worked with his father in the deep, dark pit
Many and many a year ago
Digging with his shovel, his mandrel, and his pick
For he was a collier laddie.

And when his long day's work was done
Many and many a year ago
He was too tired to walk, too tired to run
Like many a collier laddie.

His dad would lift him and carry him back
Many and many a year ago
Carry him home through the miles of dark
For he was a collier laddie.

My grandpa sat in his wooden chair
Many and many a year ago
He had bright blue eyes and snow-white hair
And he'd been a collier laddie.

He told me this tale of when he was a boy
Many and many a year ago
And worked in the darkness and never went to play
So remember the collier laddie.

## THE BLACK FERN

Here is the fossil
Preserving in anthracite
Its shining pattern            its still shape

Which in green silence
Was a fern uncurling
Beneath birdsong            under the trees

Its tender fronds were
Softer than fingers
In that young world            in the beginning

But the wind is dead
That shook its softness
And time has pressed it            in layers of years

Time has buried it
In heaviest darkness
And the living fern is            in this black rock

Touch with your fingers
The leafy fossil
The delicate statue            the coal-black fern

## THE PIT PONIES

They come like the ghosts of horses, shyly,
To this summer field, this fresh green,
Which scares them.

They have been too long in the blind mine,
Their hooves have trodden only stones
And the soft, thick dust of fine coal,

And they do not understand the grass.
For over two years their sun
Has shone from an electric bulb

That has never set, and their walking
Has been along the one, monotonous
Track of the piled coal trucks.

They have bunched their muscles against
The harness, and pulled and hauled.
But now they have come out of the underworld

And are set down in the sun and real air,
Which are strange to them. They are humble
And modest, their heads are downcast, they

Do not attempt to see very far. But one
Is attempting a clumsy gallop. It is
Something he could do when he was very young,

When he was a little foal a long time ago
And could run fleetly on his long foal's legs,
And almost he can remember this. And look,

One rolls on her back with joy in the clean grass!
And they all, awkwardly and hesitantly, like
Clumsy old men, begin to run, and the field

Is full of happy thunder. They toss their heads,
Their manes fly, they are galloping in freedom.
The ponies have come above ground, they are galloping!

# AN ODDITY OF OGRES

*IN BLACK CHASMS*

In black chasms, in caves where water
Drops and drips, in pits deep under the ground,
The ogres wait. A thousand years will not
Alter them. They are hideous, bad-tempered,
Bound only to be cruel, enemies of all.
Slow-moving, lazy, their long hard arms
Are strong as bulldozers, their red eyes
Gleam with deceit. When they smile,
It is not with kindness. In their language
They have no words for friendship, honesty,
Loyalty, generosity. Their names are
Bully, Slyness, Greed, Vandal, and Cunning.
They hate light and quarrel among themselves.
A single ogre will pass by or only threaten
In his loud, rough voice, but they are dangerous
In packs. Be on your guard against them, keep
Always a brave front, value your friends,
For they are needed against ogres.

## SONG OF THE GIANT-KILLER

Poor giant, I see you still don't know
The true identity of your foe—
    Stop roaring.
As empty vessels make most noise
You fill the whole sky with your voice.
    So boring.

I knew your grandpa, tall Goliath.
I met him on a stony path
    Before the battle.
He wasn't hard to neutralise—
I hit him once between the eyes,
    Made his bones rattle.

Then there's your uncle, Heavy Ned,
Another not to die in bed,
    Poor fellow.
I cut the beanstalk with a smile
And through the air Ned fell a mile
    On to the meadow.

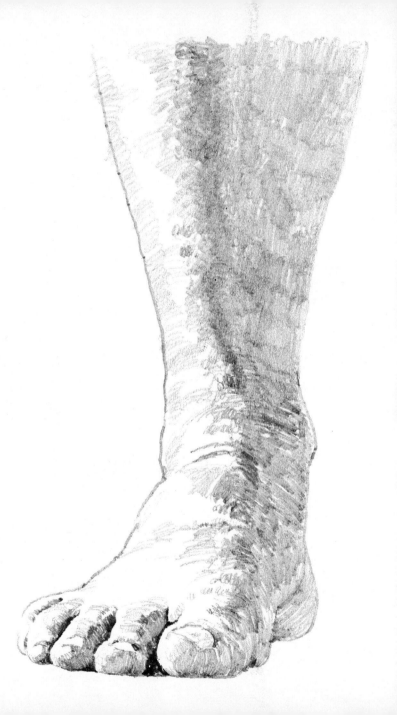

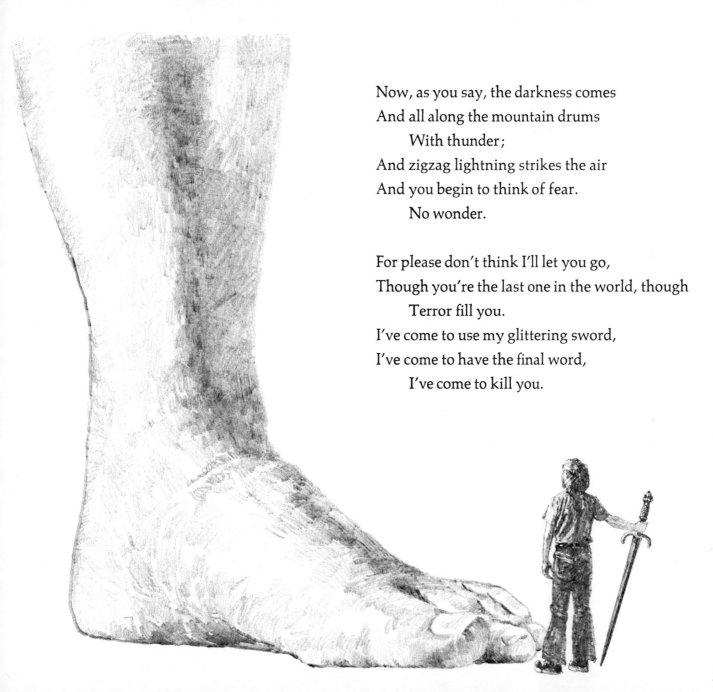

Now, as you say, the darkness comes
And all along the mountain drums
    With thunder;
And zigzag lightning strikes the air
And you begin to think of fear.
    No wonder.

For please don't think I'll let you go,
Though you're the last one in the world, though
    Terror fill you.
I've come to use my glittering sword,
I've come to have the final word,
    I've come to kill you.

33

# CHRISTMAS ANIMALS

*MICE IN THE HAY*

out of the lamplight
        (whispering worshipping)
the mice in the hay

timid eyes pearl-bright
        (whispering worshipping)
whisking quick and away

they were there that night
        (whispering worshipping)
smaller than snowflakes are

quietly made their way
        (whispering worshipping)
close to the manger

34

yes, they were afraid
    (whispering worshipping)
as the journey was made

from a dark corner
    (whispering worshipping)
scuttling together

but He smiled to see them
    (whispering worshipping)
there in the lamplight

stretched out His hand to them
    they saw the baby King
hurried back out of sight
    (whispering worshipping)

## THE STABLE CAT

I'm a Stable Cat, a working cat,
I clear the place of vermin.
The cat at the inn
       is never thin
But I am never fat.

But I don't complain of that—
I'm lithe and sleek and clever.
The mice I chase
       about the place,
For I'm the Stable Cat.

But tonight, well, things are different.
I make the small mice welcome.
I ask them all
       to pay a call
And keep my claws in velvet.

Sparrows out of the weather,
The mild, roo-cooing pigeons,
These flying bands
       are all my friends.
We're happy together.

All live things under this roof,
All birds, beasts and insects,
We look with joy
       at Mary's boy,
Are safe in His love.

## OUT ON THE WINDY HILL

Out on the windy hill
Under that sudden star
A blaze of radiant light
Frightened my master.

He got up, left our sheep,
Tramped over the moor,
And I, following,
Came to this open door,

Sidled in, settled down,
Head on my paws,
Glad to be here, away
From the wind's sharpness.

Such warmth is in this shed,
Such comfort from the Child,
That I forget my hard life,
Ignore the harsh world,

And see on my master's face
The same joy I possess,
The knowledge of peace,
True happiness.

## THE QUIET-EYED CATTLE

The quiet-eyed cattle
Are nervous and heavy
They clumsily huddle
And settle together

The mists of their breathing
Are wreathing and twining
And wisp to the window
And fade in the moonlight

Out over the meadow
Where cattle tomorrow
Will amble in pasture
And always remember

Will always remember
The King in the manger
The Child in their stable
Whose name lives forever.

## THE CAMELS, THE KINGS' CAMELS.

The Camels, the Kings' Camels, *Haie-aie*!
Saddles of polished leather, stained red and purple,
Pommels inlaid with ivory and beaten gold,
Bridles of silk embroidery, worked with flowers.
The Camels, the Kings' Camels!

We are groomed with silver combs,
We are washed with perfumes.
The grain of richest Africa is fed to us,
Our dishes are of silver.
Like cloth-of-gold glisten our sleek pelts.
Of all camels, we alone carry the Kings!
Do you wonder that we are proud?
That our hooded eyes are contemptuous?

As we sail past the tented villages
They beat their copper gongs after us.
"The windswift, the desert racers, see them!
Faster than gazelles, faster than hounds,
*Haie-aie*! The Camels, the Kings' Camels!"
The sand drifts in puffs behind us,
The glinting quartz, the fine, hard grit.
Do you wonder we look down our noses?
Do you wonder we flare our superior nostrils?

All night we have run under the moon,
Without effort, breathing lightly,
Smooth as a breeze over the desert floor,
One white star our compass.
We have come to no palace, no place
Of towers and minarets and the calling of servants,
But a poor stable in a poor town.
So why are we bending our crested necks?
Why are our heads bowed
And our eyes closed meekly?
Why are we outside this hovel,
Humbly and awkwardly kneeling?
How is it we know the world is changed?

# GOOD NIGHT

*THE SAND ROSE*

If a wind blows in the desert,
If a wind blows all day long,
If a wind full of hard sand,
Of flying grit, sand hard as diamonds,
Each grain small as a fly's eye,
If a wind blows for years,
Spitting the sand,
Multitudes of shot grains
Closer than gnats,

Faster and harder than bullets
Through a crack in the rocks,
Piling the spat dust,

The tiny quartz,
One on the other
With such ferocity

They fuse together, join,
Become a small, growing stone,
Grow, grain on grain,

Develop sand leaves, sand
Petals, a flower-heart of sand, a
Slow, opening bud—then

The Arab boys
Will search for it among crevices,
Pluck the stone flower

Formed by wind and sand,
Will sell it for a few coins
To tourists, holiday makers,

Will call it: Sand Rose.

## THE BOY IN THE STONE

The boy in the stone
lived in a quarry
nobody saw him
he lived all alone.

Nobody heard him.
He lived there unmoving
his stone voice was silent
his stone eyes were closed.

But they cut from the rock
the block of his prison.
The ton of his marble
was lifted and carried.

And chip went the sculptor
with months of his labor
with hammer and chisel
to free the stone boy.

He stepped from the stone
to stand near the fountain
his stone eyes were open
his stone mouth a smile.

The boy in the stone
an age in the quarry
lives now with water
is never alone.

## SEA AND SAND

The waves lined up
Like a military band
And marched and marched
Upon the land
    With a POMP
    And a PRIDE.

Hey, said the sand,
You can't do that,
Tripped up the waves,
Who fell down flat,
    With an oops!
    And a splash.

The sun went down
Behind a cloud,
The moon came up
And looked around,
Sea and sand
They slept sound,
    With a hush
    With a hush
    With a hush.

# MERLIN & THE SNAKE'S EGG

*MERLIN & THE SNAKE'S EGG*

All night the tall young man
    Reads in his Book of Spells,
Learning the diagrams,
    The chants and stratagems
And words to serve him well
    When he's the world's magician.
*But he needs the snake's egg.*

The night is thick as soot,
    The dark wind's at rest,
The fire's low in the grate.
    Where he lies at Merlin's feet
The black dog stirs and moans.
    Dreams trouble his sleep.
*Will they search for the snake's egg?*

For the purest of magic
    Four things must be found:
Green cress from the river,
    Gold herbs from the ground,
The top twig of the high oak,
    And the snake's round, white egg.
*Will they find the snake's egg?*

Early, before white dawn
    Disturbs the sleeping world,
Merlin is on his way
    To the forbidden wood.
Glain, the old black dog,
    Steps where his master walked.
*They go for the snake's egg.*

Glain, are yours the sharp eyes
    To see where the leaf turns?
To know that small, dark hole
    Where the mouse's eye burns?
Can your ears pick up the sound
    Of the mole's breath underground?
*Can you find the snake's egg?*

Merlin stands at the water's edge,
    At the river's flood.
He stands in the salmon's scales,
    His blood is the salmon's blood.
He swims in the slanting stream,
    In the white foam a whiter gleam.
*He has pulled the green cresses.*

Merlin stands in the wide field
    Where the small creatures hide.
His long, straight limbs are lost,
    He is changed to a spider.
He crawls on crooked legs, his head
    Moves from side to side.
*He has cropped the gold herbs.*

Merlin stands beneath the oak.
    Feathers sprout from his arms.
His nose is an owl's hooked nose,
    His voice one of night's alarms,
His eyes are the owl's round eyes,
    Silent and soft he flies.
*He has brought down the top twig.*

But Glain in the troubled wood
        Steadfastly searches.
The day's last light leans in
        Under the bushes.
And there, like a little moon,
        Pale, round, and shining,
*He has found the snake's egg.*

# Index of First Lines